C. D. Bell

# Memorial of the Clan of the Bells

more particularly of the Bells of Kirkconnel & Bells of Blackethouse, chiefs

of the name

C. D. Bell

**Memorial of the Clan of the Bells**
*more particularly of the Bells of Kirkconnel & Bells of Blackethouse, chiefs of the name*

ISBN/EAN: 9783337393021

Printed in Europe, USA, Canada, Australia, Japan

Cover: Foto ©Andreas Hilbeck / pixelio.de

More available books at **www.hansebooks.com**

# MEMORIAL

Of the Clan of

# THE BELLS,

More particularly of the

## BELLS of Kirkconnel

&

## BELLS of Blackethouse,

Chiefs of the Name.

Printed privately and only for a few Friends

MDCCCLXIV.

THE following pages are printed for the purpose of obviating the liability entailed by possession of a few scraps and sketches.

Under a vague idea of paying a compliment, those who know of such a collection may often request copies, and time and trouble must be expended if a graceful refusal cannot be substituted. Wherefore, as preferable, the cost of printing and the trouble of making woodcuts have been, once for all, incurred; and he who criticizes the primitive roughness of the latter may try to do better with a bradawl and any wood except box, or remember the proverb anent "the gift horse."

The Rammerscales MS. speaks for itself. It is now given in blackletter type, and quasi antique form; but otherwise, not even a comma has been intentionally added to or taken from the copy.

As to the Notes, a distance of some thousands of miles from probable sources of information will explain many imperfections, readily removable by any one more happily situated.

**A**

Copy of an old MS. in the Library of the last Bell of Rammerscales, said to have been written about the year 1692.

---

Memorial of the Family of Bell, more particu=larly of the Bells of Kirkconnel, now of Blackethouse, the universally acknowledged Chief of the Name.

---

**B**

SOME, who with no small curiosity have inquired into the origin of surnames, are of opinion that the Ancestors of the Ancient Family of the Bells of Kirkconnel were of French extraction; that in the Reign of King Robert the Second a gentleman called William le Bell came over to Scotland with the Earl Douglas, when he returned from an embassy to France,

**C**

anno mccclxxiv. So much is certain, that the Family settled in the great Lordship of Annan-dale and Sheriffdom of Dumfries in the South, when that Barony belonged to the Earls of Douglas. They were Vassals and Retainers of the Great House of Douglas; indeed most, if not all, of the Gentlemen of Annandale were.

**D**

THE first Charter that appears from Records and Vouchers relating to the Bells is a Charter granted by Archibald, Earl of Douglas, to William Bell, of the lands of Kirkconnel, which is ratified by a Charter under the great Seal of King James the First, anno mccccxxiv.

**I**T was this gentleman who first built a fort upon his Estate, which was called Bell's Tower. I am certainly informed that above the principal gate was cut in freestone, in a Skutcheon, three Bells, and for a Crest, a hand holding a dagger, paleways proper.

**I**T is a fact uncontroverted, the Bells of Kirkconnel were a very brave and warlike race of men, and upon all occasions they stuck firm to the House of Douglas, with whom they were allied in blood as well as their Vassals; that they generally accompanied any of the family in their expeditions and invasions into England; and the Bells of Kirkconnel being valient men, were always sent upon the most hazardous enterprises, especially on the borders, where sometimes much blood was shed and great booty was carried off from the enemies of the country.

**T**HOMAS BELL, of Kirkconnel, in the reign of James the Second, stuck firm to the unhappy James, Earl of Douglas, for, in mccccli, when the Earl went to the Court of England to concert the raising of a rebellion in Scotland, he, Thomas Bell, as one of the Earl's firm friends, accompanied him, and his name is included in the letters of safe conduct granted by the King of England for that effect; and, being involved in the Earl of Douglas's rebellion, so did this gentleman forfeit his Estate of Kirkconnel; and, if I be not much mistaken, the Estate and Castle of Bell's Tower also.

**J**

IN the reign of James the Third, upon a threatened invasion from England, mccccxxxiii, a Garrison (consisting of twenty men) was ordered to lie in Bell's Tower, and to be maintained at the charge of the Crown, a tax having been raised for that purpose.

**K**

THO' the Family lost the lands and Estate of Kirkconnel, yet they retained and kept possession of Blackethouse, in Annandale, from whence they have taken their designation; yet the memory of their being originally Lairds of Kirkconnel is still kept up, for as all the surname of Bell, throughout the king= dom, do acknowledge Blackethouse for their Chief, who they constantly own is lineal Heir, and Successor, and Representative of Bell of Kirkconnel.

**L**

THE Family of Blackethouse have always allied themselves with the Best Families of the South, as the Maxwells once, and again the John- stones, Charteris of Amisfield, Carruthers of Holemains, and the Grahames of Esk, which family is now dignified with the Title and Honour of Viscount Preston.

**M**

JOHN BELL, of Blackethouse, stood firm to King Charles the First in all his troubles. Being Governor of Carlisle, he refused to yield the city for some days, for which the Tower of Blackethouse was entirely burnt, together with the papers of the Family. Notwithstanding of that he, at the head of a flying party, cut off the stragglers of Cromwell's army.

THERE was one of the Family, Jockie Bell Brackenburn, who is interred at Kirkbankhead Churchyard, upon whose Tombstone is the following Epitaph, yet legible— N

" Here lies Jockie Bell of Brackenburn under this stane
" Five of my ain sons laid it on my wame
" Man for my meat and master for my wife
" Lived all my days without sturt or strife
" If thou be better in thy days than I have been in mine
" Take the stane off my wame, and lay it on thine.

The ingenious Dr. Pitcairn translated it into Latin verse— O

Hic Belus abscondit caput objectum per ulbam
Impiger ut qoundam saepe referre nobum
Siste domum conjux eustam surbabit et ille
Semper cura prima placere nile.

WILLIAM BELL, of Blackethouse, did lately dispose of his Estate of Blackethouse in Annandale to a re= lation and branch of his own Family, having purchased an Estate near Kelso, which he called Blackethouse, to keep up the Memory and Memorial of his Ancient designation, and was undoubted Chief of the Surname, and used the principal coat of arms of the Family, viz., Azure three Bells. P

THE surname of Bell is far spread in the West. I am informed by a gen= tleman of great veracity that a son of Kirkconnel and Blackethouse, John Bell, in the reign of King James the Fifth, came Q

with the Earl of Angus to the West, that the
Earl settled him in a possession of his own, the
lands of Cleilandtownhead, within the Barony
of Bothwell and Lordship of Lanark, where they
yet remain.

JOHN BELL, one of his name, came
and settled in the city of Glasgow
in mdcxxxviii, at the beginning of
the troubles in the reign of King Charles
the First. He died in London, mdcxli,
being one of the Commissioners of the
Treaty of Rippon, in order to settle peace
between the King and people of Scotland. He
left three Sons, James Bell, of Provosthaugh,
whose arms are (matriculated as in the Lyon
Office) viz., Azure, a fess between three bells;
crest, a Roe feeding proper; motto, Signum
Pacis Amor. From him is descended John
Bell, of Antrimony, in the county of Stirling, and the Bells who are Town Clerks of
Linlithgo.

Patrick Bell, the second son, was in the
affairs of the Magistracy of Glasgow, whose
posterity are in a flourishing condition. Patrick
Bell, of Dunsagston, is his Grandson and
Heir.

Sir John Bell, of Hamilton, from the third son,
who was formerly Provost of Glasgow, in the
reign of Charles the Second and King James the
Seventh, executed his office with great reputation
and moderation; he is still to this day remembered
as one of the worthiest Provosts that sat in the
Chair. His great grandson is a Minor, and a
promising youth.

THERE was another brother of this Ancient Family in the time of King James the Sixth, came and settled in the city of Glasgow. Robert Bell, when Mr. John Bell, was Minister at Glasgow in mdcxxxbiii, and downwards of his son, Mr. Robert Bell, descended a race of very worthy Clergymen. His lineal Heir is Mr. Robert Bell, Minister of Craiging, and of his daughter who is married to John Luke, Merchant, is descended the whole of the most opulent families of the Lukes and the Boyles in Glasgow.

THERE was another gentleman, Tevi=
otdale, designed Bell of Belford, who bought the lands of Mow, in the reign of Charles the First, from Mow of that Ilk, and named it Belford.

THERE were also Bells of Whiteside, in Galloway, who all acknowledge and acquiesce in Bell of Blackethouse as their Chief. And from Blackethouse are more lately sprung the Bells of Scots=
bridge, Starkbridge, Crowdieknows, Allin, and 'Between the Waters,' in the Parish of Mid=
dlebie and Lordship of Annandale, in the County of Dumfries.

IN Sibbald's History of Fife there is a Charter to David de Wymps, by Duncan, Earl of Fife, dated mcccxxxii, in which Thomas Bell, Citizen and Merchant, is a witness of St. Andrew's, in Wymous or Wymous Cronikil, Book biii, chap. xxbi, anno mcccxxxii.

U

**WILLIAM BELL**, a famous person, Dean of Dunkeld, was chosen Bishop of St. Andrew's, but from some opposition was never installed. He died at Rome, blind, soliciting his cause. The see was vacant nine years.

V

**FERGUS GRAHAM**, of Plump, Ancestor of the Grahams of Netherby, Lord Preston, married Siballa, daughter of William Bell, of Blackethouse.

W

**RICHARD BELL**, Prior of Durham, was twenty-fifth Bishop of Carlisle in mccclxxviii. Built Bell's Tower, see Nicholson Burns's Antiquities of Cumberland and Westmoreland.

X

**WALTER BELL** was Provost of Queen's College, Oxford, in mcccccxx.

**WILLIAM BELL** was one of the Members of Parliament for Carlisle, iii Henry b, mccccxvii—xviii.

**RICHARD BELL** was Mayor of Carlisle during the Plague, mdxcvi—xcvii.

**JOHN BELL** was Chief Baron of the Exchequer in Dumfriesshire, between md and mdc.

AMONG those who submitted to the Crown of England, in mdxlvii, the Bells of Tinwald are stated at 36/, see Nicholson Burns's History of Cumberland and Westmoreland.

———

Copy of an old MS.—written apparently about One Hundred and Sixty years ago—in the Library of the last Bell of Rammerscales.

———

Copied at Rammerscales in mdccclii.

(Signed)     J. F. A.

I BEIR TE BEL

B

# NOTES.

## A.

THE manuscript is given according to the copy, and possibly the first part of it may date from about 1692, but the interlineations or addenda of a later writer must have been incorporated with the original text, for the notice of JOHN BELL, of Antermony, relates to subsequent events; and the information given in the last six paragraphs has evidently been gathered from the work of Nicholson and Burns, on the Antiquities of Westmoreland and Cumberland, of which, it is supposed, no copy existed in 1692.

## B.

" *Some, who with no small curiosity have inquired,*" &c.

The result of such inquiries here given is brief, meagre, and unsatisfactory, but it has a great appearance of probability in its favour, inasmuch as the faint traces time has left of the condition of the shores of the Solway Firth, for some centuries prior to the Norman Conquest, tempt the inquirer to look for the origin of the name rather to the Anglo-Saxons or Anglo-Normans than to the remnant of any earlier occupants saved from destruction by their inaccessible hills or impenetrable morasses.

. "If," says the introduction to the fifth edition of Scott's Minstrelsy of the Border, "we may trust the Welsh bards in their accounts of the wars between " the Saxons and Danes of Deira and the Cumraig, imagination can hardly form " any idea of conflicts more desperate than were maintained on the borders " between the ancient British and their Teutonic invaders. Thus the Gododin " describes the waste and devastation of mutual havoc in colours so glowing as " strongly to recall the words of Tacitus, ' *Et ubi solitudinem faciunt, pacem* " *appellant.*' "

The suggestion, probably tradition, as to the first Le Bell is, therefore, entitled to much consideration; but the inquiry will naturally be, " *Was the Earl of Douglas in France in* 1374? Now, this question can only be answered by those within arm's length of acknowledged authorities; but Hume of Godscroft seems to indicate that about the year 1370, William, fifth of the name, tenth Lord and first Earl of Douglas, was one of the claimants of the crown on the death of David the Second, from which circumstance, nothing to the contrary being stated, it may be inferred that the Earl might have been too much occupied by his own affairs in Scotland for a few years to undertake, willingly, any embassy to a foreign State.

As to the name itself, there is no origin so probable as the local or territorial. Belle was a place of some importance in its day, although the name or its position may not be found in modern gazetteers or atlases. The Bibel of English Policy says :

"Also over all Scotland the commodities
"Are fettes and hydes, and of wool the fleece,
"All this must pass by us away,
"Into Flaunderes by England, this is no nay.
"And all her wool is dressed for to sell
"In the towns of Poperynge and of Belle."

In an old gazetteer available, namely, "Dictionaire Geographique Portatif. "A Bruxelles Chez Benoit le Francq, November, 1792, appeareth ' Belle voyez "Bailleul.'" But a rapid reference, in surprise, to Bailleul results in the immediate dissolution of any vague notion of a Bell alliance to the illustrious name of Balliol, for there stands

"Bailleul ou Bellé, *Balliolium*, pet. ville de Fr. dans la chât, de "même nom, au C. de Flandre, anciennement assez forte, mais "anjourd 'hui sans défense," &c., &c.

and it may be surmised that the clansman who could gravely quote that, might possibly claim descent from Philip le Bel, or even Bel and the Dragon.

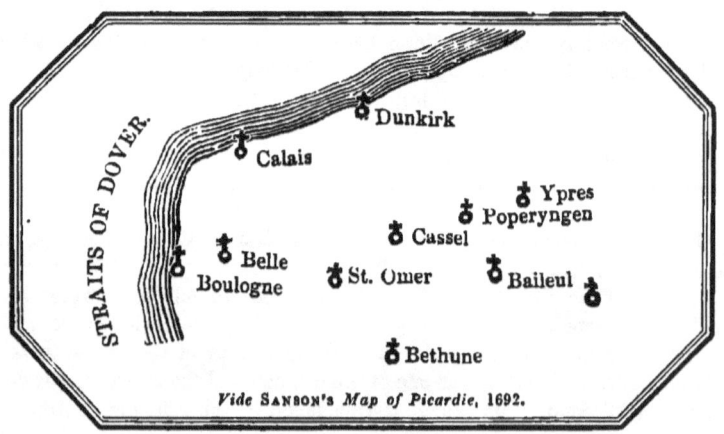

*Vide* Sanson's *Map of Picardie,* 1692.

Still old rhyme, as above quoted, proves the existence of some town without the accent (unpleasant in English) on the final letter, and one at least, printed in the same style as Poperyngue, is found in Sanson's Map of Picardie, 1692, situated about nine miles east of Boulogne Sur Mer, and on a small stream which enters the sea about a mile and a half to the north of it.

May not Belle have sent a *De Belle* across the channel as easily as the other towns of Picardy, such as Bailleul, Bethune, and Lisle produced their De Baliols, Beatons, and Lyalls? The following quotation as to the name of Ros, Rose, or Ross may show the difference between Le and De to be of no great importance, viz.: "Boethius tells that, anciently, 'Cœperunt cognamenta ab agris sumere.' "In these the surname did not give the title, but the title the surname. And "till within little more than ane age such surnames had ever the word *De* "prefixed to them; as, upon the other hand, patronimicks were written with the "genitive, as Johannes Donaldi, for MacDonald. Other surnames had the "particle Le or The prefixed, as Sir John the Graham, The Keith, The Bruce, "The Hay, &c. I have found sometimes the particle De and sometimes the "particle Le permitted to the surname (of Rose), &c., &c," vide Rose of Kilravock, Edinburgh, 1848. *Ergo*, the name might have been De Belle. It exists in that form to this day. In South Africa there is a family of Dutch or French descent called De Bell, and in Holland we have Van Belle, bearing D'azur au lion d'or, arm. et lamp. de gu; à la bord. comp. de gu et d'arg. de seize pièces; also Belle (or De Belle) in Flanders, bearing *D'or à six cloches d'azur, bataillées de gu*. Crest: *deux têtes et cols de cerf, adossées, celle à dextre d'herm, celle à sen. de c-herm*. But this last may have been resident for a time in Britain,—there being nothing, except in the Anglo-Saxon language, to connect the name of Bell with church or hawks' bells, or the belling of the stag.

A bell was also borne by the Prussian family of Bell, ennobled 1787, but now extinct. The arms were, *coupé: au 1 d'arg. au lion naiss. d'or. la queue fourchée, arm. et lamp. de gu., mouv. du coupé et tenant entre ses pattes une cloche d'arg., &c., &c.*

Among other continental armigeri of the name none bear the bell so far as is known. There are

> Bell de Schall, in the Rhenish provinces,
> Bel van den Berch, in Holland, and
> Bel de Wevelinckhoven, in the Netherlands.

There are, however, also families named Le Bel in Picardy. Others with different arms in Champagne, besides Le Bel des Aulnays and Le Bel de la Clartière, in Picardy, and Le Bel du Hommet, in Normandy. It is unnecessary to give the blazonry of their arms at length; none of them bear the bell or have reference to the stag.

℃.

*" So much is certain that the Family settled in the South when that Barony (Annandale) belonged to the Earls of Douglas."*

It is at least certain that the family were vassals or retainers of the great House of Douglas, as the author admits with an apologetical explanation to the effect that the Bells were, in that respect, no worse than most, if not all, the gentlefolk of Annandale. Had keen research in history been the fashion of his day rather than the easy credence of tradition, it might have been added in proof of the respectability of such vassalage, that the oldest known original of the Great House of Douglas was himself in earlier times a vassal—a church vassal,—named Theobaldus Flammaticus, or Theobald Fleming, who, in the year 1150, held of the Abbot of Kelso the lands of Dhu Glas, on the dark grey stream.

All vulgar tradition has a tendency to refer events to known names. The name of Douglas was probably current round every hearth long after those of Bruce, Soulis, March, and Cumyn, as powerful rulers on the border, had passed from recollection in the country side, and thus, tradition notwithstanding, it is open to much doubt that the Bells settled in Annandale so lately as in 1374. Before that date, the fashion of dropping the De, Le, or The, as a prefix to the name, prevailed in Scotland; and the early strength of the clan in Annandale, as well as its spread elsewhere, show, if it originated in a settler in Annandale of 1374, a fecundity of race utterly irreconcilable with Dr. Colenso's ideas.

Besides, there was at least one Bell in Scotland forty-two years before 1374, if we may rely on Nimmo's Chronicle, and the Charter of Duncan, Earl of Fife, of the year 1332, witnessed by Thomas Bell of St. Andrew's, quoted in the manuscript itself.

In 1404 we have traces of Bells in Blackethouse, and under Robert III., we have "carta con. given by Alexander Irvine of Drum, to Robert Bell, Burgess " of Dundee, of the wood-set of the lands of Inch Stare, and of the annual furth "of Owris," wherever and whatever that may be, "in vice com. Forfar."

A general view of all the early traces visible seems rather to give rise to the idea that the first De Belle, or Le Belle, who crossed the Channel, was a follower of some one of the Norman Barons; and that he, or a descendant, was a retainer of a Lord of the Scottish Marches, perhaps of March, or Soulis, or Comyn, who, by good luck, or insignificance, or (with due reverence be it said) by turning his coat, managed to escape forfeiture when his superiors were exiled on the fall of Baliol, or during other political changes. As in other cases further north, such as that of the Gordon or the Frazer, he may have rooted himself on the Marches, and may have bred and collected around him a fierce clan, sinking, like the Anglo-Norman beyond the Irish pale, to a condition Hybernior ipsis Hybernicis.

Against this supposition it may be urged that the name does not occur in Ragman Roll; but that is not decisive, for many names indubitably proved to have been then established and of much weight on the Marches are not therein noticed. The Bells may have been among those who are said to have retired to the mosses and hills, maintaining in these natural fastnesses a sulky independence.

<hr/>

**D.**

### " *The first Charter of Kirkconnel.*"

The authority for this statement is not given, but even if the first parchment voucher be as mentioned, it does not prove the date of first occupation. Tenure by the sword in Scotland was in many cases changed to " holding by sheepskin " at comparatively late dates, in some instances not until the reign of James the VI. Burke mentions Ettrick Forest lands thus feued for the first time in 1587 ; and for the lands of Deloraine, adjacent to Buccleugh, which, though a part of a queen's dowry, were immemorially possessed by the Scotts, a crown charter was not obtained before 1545.

Twenty years before 1424 Bell of the Blackethouse appears to have had his initials cut in freestone on the lintel of his peelhouse. They were clearly visible, in 1857, over the door of the staircase tower somewhat in this form :

**WB
1404**

The friendship or enmity of such a clan as that of Bell is supposed to have been, would of course be of some importance to the Lords of the Marches, and when the fashion of the day rendered it expedient, the chief and chieftains would have no difficulty in obtaining such vouchers as were granted to Bell of Kirkconnel ; but the lands therein mentioned may have been long previously possessed by the nominal grantee.

Kirkconnel, as a name, seems to have been rather of frequent occurrence in that part of the Marches. Several will be found mentioned in the Statistical Account of Scotland 1845,—*e.g.*, Kirkconnel, now a farm in Kirkcudbrightshire, see page 88 ; Kirkconnel Hill and Kirkconnel Moor, in the parish of Tongland, when Lag surprised Whiteside, page 87 ; and Kirkconnel on the right bank of the Nith, near its mouth, in the parish of Troqueer, also in the same county.

But the place referred to in the manuscript seems to be Kirkconnel, in the parish of the same name, now joined with that of Kirkpatrick, under the designation of Kirkpatrick Fleming, in the county of Dumfries. That is supposing the original Kirkconnel did not set the example to Blackethouse, in an effort " to keep up the memory and memorial of his ancient designation " (see note P), in which case Kirkconnel near Blackethouse and Kirkpatrick, may have acquired its name like the new Blackethouse near Kelso. The Statistical Account, page 280, informs us that in the north-west part of the parish, the mansion-house of Sprinkell stands about 200 or 300 yards to the eastward of the place where the old family residence and village of Kirkconnel stood, and in page 279, that in the burial-ground of Kirkconnel, a part of the old church, which is said to have derived its name from Connell, a Scotch saint, who flourished about the commencement of the 7th century, is still standing; but the transfer of the name would render the transfer of the tradition easy in the course of a generation or two.

"Here is the scene of the impassioned tale of 'Fair Helen of Kirkconnel Lee,'" "which has been so often told in prose and verse," that the names of Bell, Irvine, and Fleming have been frequently interchanged in the characters of hero, heroine, and assassin,—and no one can now-a-days say which was which.

## E.

### " Bell's Tower."

There may have been two places of this name,—viz., Bell's Tower, built by William Bell of Kirkconnel, and Bell's Tower at the Rose, erected by Richard Bell, 25th Bishop of Carlisle,—otherwise the Bishop may have rebuilt the original Bell's Tower; but probably "*at the Rose*," refers to some place in or near the city of Carlisle where the Bishop built a tower.

## F.

"*Above the principal gate was cut in freestone, on a skutcheon, 3 Bells, and for a crest a hand holding a dagger paleways proper.*"

As the present heraldic tincture lines were not invented when Bell's Tower was built, it is difficult to imagine how the crest was shown *proper* without painting as well as cutting the freestone; but the arms are old, as may be seen on reference to Nisbet, vol. 1, p. 437: "The name of Bell, with us, carry, "relative to their name, bells,—as Bell of Kirkconnel, *azure*, three bells *or*.— "Pont's M.S., plate ii, fig. 26."

Bell of Rammerscales, whose estate went to Macdonald, bore the same crest with the motto "I beir the bel," which looks like a rough honest original—and perhaps is—especially as it may be traced in the Latin "Fulget Virtus," translated, as many other old-fashioned mottoes have been, by genteel descendants of a race of old gentlemen. These arms are not derived from a foreign source, and they give some additional reason to doubt the date, 1374, for had a foreign gentleman then immigrated he would probably have preserved and transmitted his family bearings; but if, on the contrary, the descendant of a Norman emigrant, of a date prior to the fashion of bearing hereditary arms, assumed or was granted coat armour, when his good service and that of the clan was rewarded or their friendship secured by charter of their lands in feu under the Douglas, about the time that house rose on the ruins of the former powerful rulers of the Scottish Marches, nothing was more likely than the very simple English pun on the Norman name, and the choice of a church bell, multiplied by three, to suit a later fashion.

## G.

*" It is a fact uncontroverted, the Bells of Kirkconnel were a very brave and warlike race of men," &c.*

At the same time it is a fact like that of the alliance in blood between Douglas and Bell, of which the proofs have nearly all disappeared, or have not been thought worthy of so much notice as in the case of some other border clans.  The forfeiture of Kirkconnel, when the Black Douglas fell, and the burning of the family records in the Blackethouse by Cromwell's troopers, have left inquirers with little to assist the most earnest gaze at the thick mist time has cast over the early history of the race on the border.

Burke says : " In these times of violence and insecurity, the names of Scottish " Lairds, of small properties in the border counties, are rarely to be met with in " the public records of national transactions, except when they had the good fortune " to distinguish themselves in some of the greater battles with their English foes, " in which they were so frequently required to bear their part, for by the tenure " of their lands they were required to hold themselves always ready to obey the " summons of their sovereign to attend his host with their sons and retainers."

This is exemplified in the case of the Bells, for, although by their position and feudal obligations, Kirkconnel and the clan must have been engaged in the far greater number of border battles, at least from the days of Robert II down to the fall of the Black Douglas at Arkinholme, and although Blackethouse and the other Lairds of the name could not avoid mustering their forces in most of the succeeding struggles for more than a hundred years, including Flodden, history is silent, or nearly so, as to their deeds and their losses.

Although the Bells were engaged in the last clan fight on the borders, namely, the battle of Dryfe Sands, and although tradition gives them the credit of deciding that contest, it is only from an aged native of Lockerby that the following has been noted :

The Johnstones of Lockerbie and Jardines of Applegarth had a very bad name for rioving,—their soubriquet " Rank thieves a' " having descended to my young days.  The Maxwells had been the aggressors, by crossing the range of hills that divides Nithsdale and Annandale, and also the river Annan. The opponents met near the Dryfewater where it meanders through a piece of very flat land before joining the Annan.

An abrupt ridge rises on the Lockerbie side of the flat named " Torwood Muir," and the site of the fray is still known by two very high natural thorns, known as Maxwell's Thorns, about two miles from Lockerbie, the only wood on Dryfe Sands.  The Maxwells and the Johnstones, and their friends, had fought until they were nearly exhausted, when the appearance of the Bells of Middlebie, coming over the rising ground to the assistance of the latter, saved the Johnstones.

The frosh men meeting the Maxwells too much exhausted to fly may account for the fearful slashing across the face that originated the phrase "*a Lockerbie*

c

*lich.*" In the Statistical Account of Scotland, county Dumfries, parish of Applegarth and Sibbaldbie, it will be found that a venerable thorn, called "the Abdie Thorn," stands in a field within 500 yards of the church. It, it is said, was planted on the spot where Bell of Abdie fell while in pursuit of the Maxwells, after the battle of Dryfe Sands. A similar memorial marks the spot, about half a mile distant in Dryfesdale parish, where it is said Lord Maxwell himself, at that time Warden of the Western Marches, was killed. The events of that day may be nothing to boast of. They are merely noticed here in illustration of the fact that, with better advantages as regards recorders, or with recorders more interested in the clan, the Bells might have made a better figure in detailed histories of the Scotch Marches at least.

In popular poetry we may see from the old Ballad of Adam Bell, Clem of the Cleugh, and William of Cloudeslye, that in very early times the surname was considered appropriate to a fierce mosstrooper or daring forrester.

In Percy's Reliques one version of the ballad is preserved. It is so well known that it is unnecessary, and so long that it is inconvenient, to quote it here. William, contrary to advice, visited his wife, was betrayed, captured, and rescued from Carlisle by Adam and Clem, who slaughtered the justice and sheriff in approved style,—afterwards visited the Court and astonished His Majesty by such incredible shooting as procured them pardon, patronage, and places about the palace, where they lived and died happily.

A document of more reliable character relative to the battle of Solway Moss mentions one of the name, then on the English side, and gives him such a place in the public records of national transactions as is alluded to by Burke. The following is an extract from a list of "*the names of the noblemen and gentlemen "of Scotland, prisoners (battle of Sollom Moss) to be sent to the King's Majesty "by Sir Thomas Wharton, Knight, with the names of their takers, as followeth:*

*      *      *      *

"*Oliver Sinkeler, one of the King of Scots' Privy Council,—Willie Bell his taker.*"

It has not been ascertained whether the chief of the name took open part against, or merely shared in the dogged discontent of the Scottish army regarding the royal favourite,—nor has any clue been found to a further description of this Willie Bell, who it seems had the good fortune to capture the cause of the disgraceful disaster by which the Scottish arms were that day sullied, and by which the heart of King James the Fifth was broken.

〰〰〰〰〰〰〰〰〰〰

𝔥.

"*The Bells of Kirkconnel being valiant men, were always sent upon the most hazardous enterprises especially on the borders.*"

Sometimes the Bells were sent elsewhere, as, for example, the Raid of Stirling, 1571. Bannatyne's Journal records that "the fourt of September, they "of Edinburgh, horsemen and futmen (and, as was reported, the most part of "Clidisdaill, that pertinet to the Hamiltons), come to Striveling, the number of

" iii or iiii C men, on hors bak, *guydit be ane George Bell,* their hac butteris
" being all horsed, entered in Striveling, be fyve houris in the morning (whair
" thair was never ane to mak watche), crying this slogane, 'God and the
" Queen! ane Hamiltoune! think on the Bishop of St. Androis, all is owres;'"
&c., &c.

" The Regent was shot by ane Captain Cader, wha confessed that he did it *at*
" *commande of George Bell,*" &c.

The introduction to the fifth edition of Sir Walter Scott's Minstrelsy of the
Scottish Border contains a lengthened notice of the affair, and observes that
hardly does our history present another enterprise so well planned, so happily
commenced, and so strangely disconcerted.

On the borders some of the clan appear to have occasionally given trouble to
their wardens, in a manner disapproved of by their countrymen in more settled
districts. Sir David Lyndsay, in a drama, makes " *Common Thift*" say :

> " Adew! my bruthir Annan thieves,
> That holpit me in my mischieves,
> Adew! Grossars, Niksonis, and Bells,
> Oft have we fairne owrthreuch the fells," &c.

Satchell, however, draws a distinction ; and the Bells, like the Armstrongs,
may have merely been

> " Able men,
> Somewhat unruly, and very ill to tame,
> I would have none think that I call them thieves,
> For if I did it would be arrant lies.
> *       *       *       *
> Near a border frontier in the time of war,
> There's ne'er a man but he's a freebooter," &c., &c.

The reprisals of those who took the law into their own hands when they
found that laws of the land could not protect them, and when the weakness of
their own monarch even subjected them to legal punishment by their foes, under
royal authority, must be regarded with a lenient eye. On the borders such
deeds were looked upon as honourable,—the more hazardous, the more
honourable.

Extracts from one document are here given in illustration of these remarks :

> " A Breviate of attempts of England, committed upon the West Marches
> " by the West Borders of Liddesdale, and fouled by the Commissioners
> " of Berwick for lack of appearance."

> " *West Marches against Liddesdale.—Martinmas,* 1587.

> " The poor widow and inhabitants of the town of Temmon complained upon
> " Laird of Mangerton, Laird of Whitaugh, and their complices, for the murder
> " of John Tweddel, Willie Tweddel, and Davie Bell ; the taking and carrying
> " away of John Thirlway, Philip Thirlway, Edward Thirlway, John Bell of
> " Clowsegill, David Bell," &c., &c.

" *West Marches of England against West Marches of Scotland.—June*, 1586.

"Geordie Taylor, of the Bone Riddings, complains upon Will Bell Redcloak, "Wat Bell, Ritchie Bell, and their complices, for 30 kine and oxen; insight "100£ sterling."

### " *June*, 1586.

"Walter Grame, William Grame, and the tenants of Esk, against Will Bell "Redcloak, Wattie Bell, and the surnames of the Carleill, for burning of their "mills, houses, corn; insight 400£."

### "18 *June*, 1586.

"William Grame, of Sleddels, against Will Bell Redcloak, Tom Bell, and "their complices, for 30 kine and oxen, 60 sheep; insight 100£ sterling."

### "26 *June*, 1586.

"James Grame and Hutchin Grame, of Peretree, against Will Bell Redcloak, "Tom Bell, and their complices, for 60 kine and oxen, 100 sheep, and the spoil "of their houses; 100£."

### " *West Marches of Scotland against West Marches of England.*

"Friends of Adam Carleill and the Bells complain upon Walter Grame, of "Netherby, Davie and Willie his brother, Richie's Will, Rob of the Fald, for "burning of Goddesbrigg, 3000 kine and oxen, 4000 sheep and gate, 500 horses "and mares; estimated to 40,000£ Scots."

The Laird of Goddesbrigg was one of the Bells (see note V). Redcloak must have had "a merry time of it" in the month of June, 1586.

This note might be much extended by notices of the rather notorious Grahams, of Peartree, and others,—as illustrative of Border life in those days, —and by extracts from various documents, from Acts of Parliament downwards; but it would lead to — no end of a printer's bill.

---

### E.

" *Thomas Bell, of Kirkconnel, in the reign of James II, stuck firm to the unhappy James Earl of Douglas," &c.*

The following is a copy of the letters of safe conduct, from Rhymer's Foedera, Ann. D. 1451. Au. 29, II. 6.

#### *Pro Comite de Douglass et Aliis.*

Rex per Literas suas patentes, per unum Annum duraturas, suscepit in salvum et securum Conductum Suum, ac in Protectionem, Tuitionem, et Defensionem suas Speciales:

> Willielmum Comitem Douglas
> Jacobum de Douglas, Militem
> Archebaldum de Douglas, Comitem de Murrawe

Hugonem de Douglas, Comitem de Ormond
Alexandrum Hume, Militem
Jacobum Dominum Hamylton, Militem
Willielmum Meldrum, Militem
Willielmum Laudre de Halton
Thomam de Cranstone
Audriam Ker de Aldtoneburn
Jacobum de Douglas de Ralston, Militem
Alanum de Kerthkert
David Hume, Militem
Johannem Rosse, Militem
Georgium de Hoppringill
Alexandrum de Hoppringill
Willielmum Balze
Georgium de Halyburton
Marcum de Halyburton
Alanum de Lawdre
Carolum de Murrase
Thomam Boll
Thomam Grahame
Jacobum de Dunbar
Robertum Heris
Willielmum Grerson
Johannem Menzies
Jacobum de Douglas
Johannem Haliburton
Magistrum Adam de Archinlok
Magistrum Johannem Clere
Thomam Ker
et Jacobum Ker.

In Regnum Regis Angliæ, ac Villam et Marchias Calesii, ac alia Loca et Dominia Regi Subjecta, cum sexaginta et septem persones in comitiva sua, Nobilibus et aliis (cujuscumque nationis seu status fuerint), Armatis vel non Armatis, et totidem equis, vel aliis Animalibus, seu infra, necnon Auro, et Argento Monetatis vel non Monetatis, Jocalibus, Vasis, Sarcinis, Fardellis, Bogeis, Literis Clausis et Patentibus, Instructionibus, Memorialibus, Libris, Bonis, et Rebus suis uteusilibus, licitis quibuscumque, sibi necessariis, tam per Terram quam per Mare, &c., prout in cæteris de conductu Literis.—Dat. Duodecimo Die Maii, 1451, Hen. 6.

And so Kirkconnel, true to his chief, was on the losing side at Arkinholme and Burnswark, where others of the former vassals of the Black Douglas fought against him under the banner of Angus; Maxwells, Johnstones, Scotts, and many more. It was a turn of the tide which, taken at the flood, led them to fortune, to the Dukedoms, Marquisates, and Earldoms of later days,—with historians to record and minstrels of the North to sing of the deeds of their ancestors,—while the name of Bell sank, until, in the days of James the VI, they were a broken clan, without power or influence enough to reward the praises that might have rescued the names of their fathers from oblivion, and for whose conduct it was doubtful whether their chief, or reputed chief of Blackethouse, could be fairly held responsible.

To the winners the royal favour was liberally shown. The possessions of the vanquished Black Douglas, and his adherents, were distributed with a lavish hand among those who turned against him in his day of distress. Maxwell gained Kirkconnel; Johnstone became Laird of Pittinane; and to Scott, of Kirkurd, ancestor of Buccleugh, the King granted Abingtown, Phareholm, and Glentonan Craig. Broad lands were also won by the chiefs of the Hamiltons, the Beattisons, and others; and the ruin of the friends of James, ninth of the name, last Earl of Douglas, 18th Lord of the same, and sixth Duke of Touraine, was complete. Those who survived became outlawed and landless men. He died a monk in the abbey of Lindores.

It may be that these more prosperous names can claim a higher origin, and an earlier place in the national and local records. The Maxwells may descend from Maccus, the follower of David, who, in the 12th century, had his grant of Maccusville on the Tweed. The Scotts may come from the man who caught a buck in a cleugh, soon enough to give them much importance, in the days of the early Kings of Scotland. The Hamiltons may have descended of the conqueror's friend, the Earl of Liecester, and may have been introduced by their relative, William the Lion. The Kers were probably of importance on the borders six hundred years ago; and so may the Johnstones, and Beattisons, and others, have been. With equal time, talents, opportunities, and diligence in earlier days, or it may be even now, available in research as to the origin and early position of the Bells, the Clan might have made a better appearance than it does in this memorial.

## J.

*" Garrison in Bell's Tower, in the Reign of James III."*

No historical record of this has been found.

## K.

*" The Family lost Kirkconnel, retained Blackethouse; Blackethouse is the acknowledged representative."*

It will be seen from the note D that there were Bells in Blackethouse probably more than twenty years before the date of the confirmation of the Charter of Kirkconnel; but it does not, therefore, necessarily follow that this statement of the mutual relation of the houses is incorrect. Kirkconnel and Blackethouse may have been held by one owner, or by different branches of the same family,—or Kirkconnel may have been a cadet of Blackethouse, judging from dates, or *vice versâ* as here stated, knowing how insufficiently some charters prove dates of first possession.

The Blackethouse is situated in the parish of Middlebie, which, says the Statistical Account of Scotland, "has long been celebrated for its families of the "name of Bell, so much so that the Bells of Middlebie became a common "expression in Dumfriesshire, and many of the most celebrated individuals of the "name, in various departments of society, may be traced to an original connection "with our parochial district. These families have mostly now become extinct "in the parish; but the prevalence of the name in a former age is testified by "the figure of a bell found on a great proportion of our grave-stones." It is provoking that no amount of writing, or guarantee as to expense, can procure a sketch or photograph of these grave-stones.

Elsewhere it is noted, " a mile distant from Sprinkell. on the right bank of "the Kirtle, is the Tower of Blackethouse, in Middlebie, formerly possessed by "a family of the name of Bell "

Again: " Nor, considering the subject of antiquities can I pass over in silence "the Tower of the Blackethouse still standing, though fast sinking into ruins — "which, like several others in the neighbouring parishes, is supposed to be one "of those forts of defence which were used in the wars between the English and "Scottish Borderers."

The following are from very rough sketches made in 1857, during the few minutes available for a passing look at the ruins, which the present proprietor has had gentlemanlike feeling enough to preserve with due care, as an interesting ornament to his elegant modern residence, although within a hundred yards of it.

The plan shows a tower with a turnpike stair in it, the only part roofed, and the walls of some building behind it indicated by the shaded part The double lines show the upper and lower edges of the slopes,

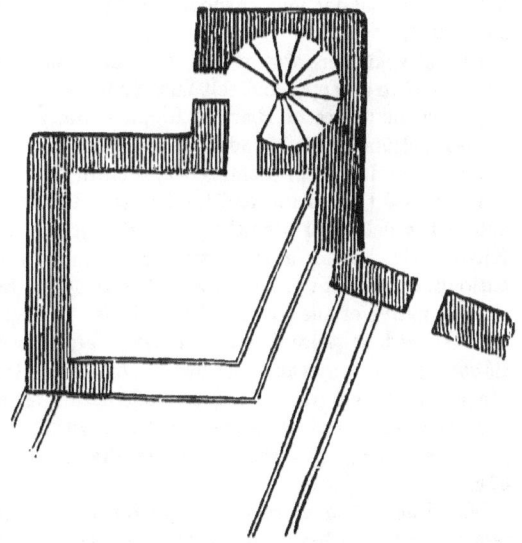

between higher and lower levels, of what may have been the floors,—or rubbish within the building now trimmed and neatly turfed with much good taste.

These floors may be traced in the sketch from the inside, which is here given, although great liberties have been taken with the trees and foliage that shade and decorate the grey walls.

Any of the clan who can afford about three hours' detention on the railway between Carlisle and Edinburgh may see the place itself without difficulty,—that is, if they are going that way at any rate, and have a "Shank's Nag," reasonably sound, at their service. At the small station of Kirtle Brig, where they should leave the train, there is neither vehicle nor hack to be had for love or money, if the neighbourhood be not much improved since 1857.

In that year there was one of the name whose beard had sprouted, and had been toned to a pepper and salt hue, under a southern sun, but who had not forgotten the names of Blacket Rig, and Blackethouse, of Annandale, in the stories told him in his boyhood, in a shire much further north, at the winter's hearth, or under the blossoming whins on the lowin side of a know. He had again crossed the equator and the border. He had seen his own calf ground; and he had delivered his ticket and valise to the solitary corduroyed porter at Kirtle Brig, having at last, after much inquiry among the learned in local antiquities and history, been directed so to do at the Carlisle station by a kind clerk, a native of the parish of Middlebie. A walk of about half an hour to the eastward, as pointed out by him-of-the-corduroys, led along pleasant roads, through green hedges and past decent cottages, to the avenue of the place so long sought for. There was an elegant modern villa residence, somewhat Elizabethan in style, as far as can be recollected, for in truth it was not honoured by a second glance of the eye so earnestly bent on the few old dark ivy-covered remnants of ruin.

Notwithstanding equally unjustifiable misrepresentation of the picturesque remains and fresh beauty of the scene, a réchauffé of the few pencil dashes made outside the walls on the same occasion is also now given, as conveying some idea (better than nothing) of the last old "stam haus" of the Bells, of which a vestige can be traced at the present day.

The sun had long sunk, and the carpet bag and pillow were yet to be sought for in some distant unknown locality vaguely described by Old Corduroy. One hurried rush down the steep bank was all that time allowed. Down through the stems of the healthy-looking lofty trees to see the fresh clear burn that rippled and murmured as it did of old, four centuries and a half ago, within ear-shot of the tower, while yet W B might

have admired his own initials and the Arabic numerals 1404 as something very fine, but, at the same time, something beyond what he probably professed to know much of. And small blame to him. There is even now a lingering and uncomfortable suspicion that some prying "howkin creature" of an antiquary may carp about a preference by monks and masons, in the 15th century, of Roman to Arabic numerals. Anyhow, that question did not disturb the enthusiasm of the Returned Exile, in the fine summer gloamin, when he viewed both the initials and the numerals with as much faith as he would have given to Mantell's Medals of Creation in like stone,—and thought he had found a deeper root in his native soil.

A printer has types to express notes of interrogation and surprise. Oh! why has he nothing to convey conventionally the idea of a groan, that it might be printed here as some relief to one who detests humbug and mere bookmaking, yet is compelled to supply these two pieces of unmitigated "gag" simply for the better paging of woodcuts.

Still some lines of blank? Talk of Nigger Drivers!!! Shall that bone last thrown to the antiquaries of the clan be further picked? No. There are no works of authority at hand, and no acquired knowledge sufficient to render them unnecessary. Shall the beauty of the banks of the Kirtle be expatiated on? No. That would require a hundred pages at least, while the printer's present requirements may be fully met by a brief assurance that if the clansman who undertakes the pilgrimage to these early haunts of the race be blessed with a partner or companions incapable of adequately appreciating the sources of his enjoyment, he may yet rely on visiting scenes of natural beauty there, such as may amply compensate any of their concessions to his peculiar tastes.

D

## 𝕷.

*" Blackethouse always allied with best families of the South."*

The only trace of these alliances of Blackethouse which has been found is of that with the Grahames of Esk, hereinafter noted (see V). The manner of stating it here, and subsequently, seems to indicate the composite nature of the manuscript as now given.

---

## 𝔐.

*" John Bell, Governor of Carlisle.   Blackethouse burnt."*

 Nowhere in Burns and Nicholson, or in other histories, can a corroboration of these statements be found,—but on the outside of the lintel of the doorway in the side wall, shown in the foregoing sketches of the Blackethouse, may be seen (or, at least, was to be seen in 1857) the letters and date as in the margin.

J. B. may refer to a rebuilding of the house, by the quondam Governor of Carlisle, after the restoration of Charles II,— and the other initials may have been those of his wife in the usual fashion of the day.

---

## 𝔑.

*" Jockie Bell, Brackenburn."*

Another version is to be found in the "Collection of Epitaphs and Monumental " Inscriptions, chiefly in Scotland, published,— Glasgow, D. McVean; Edinburgh, " Thomas Stevenson, 1834, p. 27 :

*" Inscription on John Bell."*

" John Bell lived in Annandale, on the Scots side, and has a stone 200 years old on him, with this inscription,

> " I Jocky Bell, o' Brackenbrow, lyes under this stane,
> Five of my awn sons laid it on my wame,
> I lived aw my days but sturt or strife,
> Was man o' my meat and maister o' my wife.
> If you done better in your time than I done in mine,
> Take the stane aff my wame and lay it on thine."

John Bell's monument is in Reid Kirkyard, now in the parish of Graitney.

## ⊙.

### "*Hic Belus abscondit*," *&c.*

Is this a translation? Is it verse? Is it good Latin?

Speaking from recollection and experience it may be asserted that, forty years ago, there was one school in which, had the ingenious Dr. Pitcairn been a small pupil, he could not have had a comfortable seat for at least forty minutes after tendering such a production to the master. But the

> " Maldrara dum dragos mairia laghshita largos,
> Spalando spados sive nig fig knightite gnaros," &c., &c.

of Macduff's Cross shows how a dead language may be mangled by tradition; and if verbal communications corrupt good Latin in some cases, it may be that in .others, such as this, the faults can be ascribed to cramp handwriting rather than to the reputed author.

The provoking part of the matter is that no reasonable guess at the original can be offered. It remains an unsolved puzzle.

## ℗.

### "*Blackethouse near Kelso.*"

It is supposed that the attempt to keep up the memory and memorial of this ancient designation was futile, for nothing can be heard of any Blackethouse near Kelso from several natives of that neighbourhood, or traced in the pages of the Statistical Account. It is unknown whether the sale of Blackethouse on the Kirtle was prior to 1692, or whether the name of the purchaser was Bell,— although probably it was, as he is mentioned as a relative and branch of the family of Blackethouse,—but the following initials and date were seen, in 1857, on the inside of the lintel of the doorway in the side wall of the tower,—viz :

| 17 | C B | I K | 14 |

## ⊙.

### "*Bell far spread in the West.*"

There may still be Bells in the west, or elsewhere, who can trace from Cleilandtownhead; and this notice of descent from Kirkconnel and Blackethouse may interest them.

The whole of Bothwell and Lanark is missing from the only copy of the Statistical Account of Scotland within reach,—and, consequently, no information as to the present ownership of Cleilandtownhead, or other lands in the vicinity, can be herein given.

Of course, the style of mentioning the family merely indicates the descent from Kirkconnel, through Blackethouse; but the connection with, and grant of land from Angus raises, with the other circumstances, an idea that, in the reign of the Second James, the properties were held by separate owners of the same family; and that, while Kirkconnel stuck firm to the unhappy Black Douglas, Blackethouse may have adhered to the more fortunate Red. In fact, one lost much and the other won a little in a very old game of Rouge-et-Noir. The family may have "hedged," as others are known to have done in like circumstances, down to 1745.

## R.

*"John Bell, of Glasgow, Commissioner of the Treaty of Rippon."*

Corroboration of this statement, if correct, can no doubt be easily obtained by many; but there is none in the sources of information here available. Burke records the arms of Bell of Provosthaugh exactly as blazoned, and the following notice of his descendant, of "*Antrimony*," is extracted from the *Encyclopædia Britannica:* "John Bell, of Antermony, a Scottish traveller in the first half of " the last century. He was born in 1691, and was educated for the medical " profession, in which he took the degree of M.D. In 1714 he set out for St. " Petersburg, nominated medical attendant to Valensky, recently appointed to " the Persian embassy, with whom he travelled, from 1715 to 1722, through " Russia, Turkey, Persia, and China. He had scarcely rested from this last " journey, when he was summoned to attend Peter the Great in his perilous " expedition to Derbend and the Caspian Gates. The narrative of this journey " he has enriched with interesting particulars of the public and private life of " that remarkable prince. In 1738 he was sent by the Russian Government on " a mission to Constantinople, to which, accompanied by a single attendant who " spoke Turkish, he proceeded in the midst of winter and all the horrors of " a barbarous warfare,—and in May, 1738, he returned to St. Petersburg. It " appears that after this he was several years established as a merchant at " Constantinople, where he married in 1746. In the following year he retired " to his estate of Antermony, in Scotland,—where he lived in ease and affluence, " beloved by his neighbours, and respected by all who knew him. He died in " 1780. His travels, published at Glasgow in 2 vols. 4to, 1763, were speedily " translated into French, and widely circulated in Europe."

These dates bring down the information given in the MS. to a period much later than 1692, and probably the notice of the great grandson of Sir John Bell, of Hamilton, does the same. It is left uncertain whether Robert Bell, of Glasgow, the progenitor of the race of worthy clergymen, was a brother of the

ancient family of Bell generally, or of Kirkconnel and Blackethouse in particular,
or of the Commissioner of the Treaty of Ripon. The Lukes and the Boyles
may have the inclination, and may, perhaps, still possess the means of
investigating the matter.

$$\mathfrak{S}.$$

### "*Bell, of Belford, in Teviotdale.*"

This gentleman gave an improved name to his acquired property, and since
that time further alteration seems to have taken place, for the only trace on the
local maps within reach appears to be Belford Hill. The following record,
however, is permanently fixed in Durie's decisions:

"*Bell*, contra the *Laird of Mow*, p. 743, January 22, 1635.

"The L. Mow having Wodset his Lands to one *Bell*, who Setting the Lands
"in Back-Tack, for payment of a Back Tack Duty, and after the decease of the
"L. *Mow*, Arresting the Duties of the Lands in the Tenuents hands, and
"Pursuing them thereupon, to make them forthcoming; *Nisbet*, Relict of the
"Laird *Mow*, who was Life-reuter of the Lands, before the Wodset, compearing,
"and Defending with her said Right, the Pursuer Replying, that she had
"consented to the Contract of Wodset, and producing the Contract, with her
"Subscription at the same, with an Act extracted out of the Sherif Registers
"of *Tividale*, subscribed by the clerk thereof, bearing *That she compeared
"Judicially in Judgement before the Sheriff, and Subscribed the said Contract out
"with the presence of her Husband, and made Faith, that she consented thereto
"Voluntarly, and Ratified the same*. And she Duplying, that that Act nor the
"Warrand of the same, was not subscribed by her, and was but the Assertion of
"a Nottar, and her Alledged Subscription at the Contract, not being done before
"Witnesses, and no Witnesses being Insert thereto, it was null, and so could not
"prejudge her. And the Pursuer Replying, that although there were no
"Witnesses Insert to her Subscription, yet seeing the Judicial Act produced bore
"*her to have subscribed the same in Judgement, and that she had Judicially
"Ratified the same*, it is enough to sustain the Contract, and is more than if
"there were Witnesses Insert. The *Lords* found not this Act sufficient to
"denude the Woman, and to verifie her consent, nor yet her Subscription of the
"Contract, seeing it bore, *not to be done, and Subscribed by her before Witnesses;*
"seing the same Contract Subscribed (as it bore) by her, ought to have made
"mention, that she Subscribed the same before Witnesses, who ought to have
"been insert in the Contract, and to have proported that she should have
"Subscribed the same before them; but Found that the Party might condescend
"upon the Witnesses, their Names, who saw her Subscribe the same, and that
"yet they might declare the same; But that it was not enough, that the Act
"declared that she Subscribed the same Judicially, but that he should condescend

" upon the Witnesses present, before whom she Subscribed it, and abide at the " same in that manner. Actor ——, Alter *Gilmor, Scot* Clerk," &c.

Among the Commissioners of Supply—Queen Anne's first Parliament—is mentioned, "Nithsdale and Dumfries, John Bell, of Crowdie know."

When the manuscript was in the press it was not known here that a Bell of Whiteside had been a distinguished character, otherwise he would have had a letter and note to himself. The others, with the exception of Between the Waters, may at once be disposed of as untraceable in any local map or other publication within reach.

There are many clansmen whose hearts would warm more, and whose pulses would beat faster when they read of the martyr, for his faith, of their own name, than when they peruse the most glowing record of the unswerving fidelity of Kirkconnel, or the wild assertion of natural right against oppressive power in the character of Blackethouse and his clan, including even Redcloak. To such clansmen who wisely, as regards human progress, look with more respect at a portrait in a Geneva band than on that of a warrior in a steel gorget, the following extracts may be some incentive to further inquiry and record,—see Statistical Account of Scotland, 1845, Kirkcudbright, p. 16:

" Sir Robert Grierson, of Lag, surprised John Bell, of Whiteside, and some " others on the hill of Kirkconnel, in the parish of Tongland, and barbarously " ordered them to be put to death. He would not allow their bodies to be " buried. Mr. Bell was the only son of the heiress of Whiteside, who, after the " death of his father, had married Viscount Kenmure. This nobleman met " Lag in company with Graham, of Claverhouse, in the street of Kirkcudbright, " Kenmure accused Lag of cruelty, and he retorted in highly offensive language, " which so provoked the Viscount that he drew his sword and would have run " it through the body of the persecutor," &c. (but didn't ! ! !)

See also Anworth Parish, page 377: " He" (Whiteside) " had been forfeited " in 1680, in consequence of his having been engaged at the Battle of Bothwell " Bridge. In 1685, Bell, with Halliday of Mayfield, Lennox of Irelandtown, " and two others, were surprised by Grierson of Lag, on Kirkconnel Muir, " parish of Tongland, and barbarously shot on the spot without so much as " allowing them to pray, though earnestly desired." See Wodrow's History, vol. iv, pp. 241 and 242. " Bell was buried in the churchyard of Anworth."

NOTE.—" The monument erected to his memory, and still carefully preserved, " bears the following inscription : Here lyes John Bell, of Whyteside, who was " barbarously shot to death in the paroch of Tongland, at the command of Grier " of Lag, anno 1685."

> " This monument shall tell posterity
> That blessed Bell, of Whyteside, here doth lye,
> Who, at command of bloody Lag, was shot,
> A murder strange which should not be forgot.
> Douglas, of Morton, did him quarters give,
> Yet cruel Lag would not let him survive.

This martyr sought some time to recommend
His soul to God before his days should end;
The tyrant said, What, dev'l yo've pray'd enough,
This seven long years on mountain and in cleuch;
And instantly caused him, with other four,
Be shot to death upon Kirkconnel Moor;
So thus did end the lives of these dear saints,
For their adherence to the covenants."

As a counterbalance we have, however, a Bell on the other side who is noticed with highly-spiced sectarian vituperation,—see Statistical Account of Scotland, Berwickshire, Westruther, page 70, for a note on Mr. Thomas Bell, a Presbyterian renegade, a man who was born of the meaner sort of gentry, and who deserves not to be dragged from the obscurity in which his name is buried.

## T.

*" Thomas Bell, Citizen and Merchant, of St. Andrews."*

Although no copy of Sibbald is at hand, there is, from recollection, no doubt that this reference to it and to its quotation from Nimmo's Chronicle is "*all right.*" The date, 1332, fixes the inquiring clansman on the horns of a dilemma. It indicates two or more original settlers of the name, or that the tradition in the MS. is post dated, and that the original De Belle or Le Belle of Annandale, or his "forebears," came from Picardy long before 1374. On the whole, except as a curious subject of inquiry, it does not much matter to any of us, for all who know the usual period of a generation and the laws of geometrical progression can calculate that, barring clan intermarriages, it is in vain to boast in 1864 of more than about the sixty-five thousandth part of any virtues as inherited in the blood of one ancestor of the middle of the fourteenth century, except by reasoning on homœopathic principles as to increased power through infinitesimal dilution.

## U.

*" William Bell, Dean of Dunkeld."*

This statement must be capable of verification by those who have access to any extensive collection of historical records. *The vacancy in the See probably from 1332 ... 1341. ... &c.*

## V.

*" Fergus Graham, of Plump, married Siballa, daughter of William Bell of Blackethouse."*

Burke says, "Fergus Graham, of Plump, married Sibill, daughter of William " Bell, Esquire, of God's Brigg. She was mother of—I. Sir Richard Graham of " Esk,—II. Sir George Graham, and—III. Sir Richard Graham, created 1680

" Viscount Preston." The paragraph fixes the date of a part of the manuscript between 1680, the creation of this peerage, and 1739, the year when Charles, the third Viscount, died *sine prole*.

~~~~~~~~~~~~~~~~~~~~~~~~~~~

### ᛟᛗᛚ.

" *Richard Bell, Prior of Durham, 25th Bishop of Carlisle in* 1478."

The following is from a rubbing of this churchman's tombstone and brass in the centre of the Cathedral of Carlisle,—much of the elaborate detail being, of course, omitted for want of space. The size of the original is about 10 x 6 feet.

Nothing seems to be now known of his descent from, or connection with any of the principal branches of the clan.

Nicholson and Burns merely say in the list of Bishops, "25. Richard Bell, "prior of Durham, was by the Pope's command consecrated by his predecessor, "and had the temporalities restored to him 24th April, 1478. Before he was "Bishop he had been several times one of King Edward the Fourth's Commis- "sioners in Treaties with those of the King of Scots. He built the Tower at "Rose, which still bears the name of Bell's Tower. He died in 1496, and was "buried in his own Cathedral, under the litany desk, where is his portraiture "in his pontificals drawn at full length On a brass plate are some rude Latin "verses, and on a brass margin about the stone: ' Hic Jacet Reverendus Pater "'Ricardus Bell, quondam Episcopus Karliolensis qui ab hac luce migravit "'vicesimo quarto die.———Anno Domini——— omnium defunctorum.'"

The above woodcut and description alike convey a very inadequate idea of this interesting memorial. The Latin verses are not more rude than others of that date, and the details of the pontificals are acknowledged by ecclesiastical anti- quaries to be among the most perfect of any left to us.

Since note E was printed a friend who has seen it says that Rose Castle is the name of the residence of the Bishops of Carlisle.

### ℱ.

"Walter Bell, Provost of King's College, Oxford, 1420.
"William Bell, Member of Parliament for Carlisle, 1417—18.
"Richard Bell, Mayor of Carlisle, 1696—97.
"John Bell, Chief Baron of the Exchequer in Dumfriesshire, 1500—1600."

John Bell's arms are given by Burke thus: Bell (Lord Chief Baron of the Exchequer, who died 1577), sa. a fesse erm. betw. three church bells, ar.

The information is evidently a mere note from Nicholson and Burns' History of Cumberland and Westmoreland,—or, at all events, it must have been derived from the same source. Following the example, the memorial might now be considerably enlarged by references to well-known publications.

From the *Encyclopædia Britannica* and others we may have:

"Andrew Bell, D.D., a clergyman of the English Church, who is well known "for his philanthropic efforts in the cause of education, and more particularly for "his success in extending the monitorial system of instruction in schools. He "was the projector and founder of those admirable institutions called national "schools, and the author of an experiment in education at the Male Asylum, "Madras, and of instructions for conducting schools on the Madras system, "&c., &c. Dr. Bell was born at St. Andrews in 1753, and received his education "in the university there. Some of his early years were spent in America, and "he was afterwards chaplain to Fort St. George, and minister of St. Mary's, at "Madras. During his residence in the East Indies he acquired considerable "property; which, together with some lucrative preferments in England, enabled

E

" him to bequeath no less than £120,000 in support of national institutions and " public charities. This benevolent man died at Cheltenham in 1832, and his " remains were interred in Westminster Abbey. To the liberality of Dr. Bell, " St. Andrews is indebted for the foundation of Madras College."

Benjamin Bell, an eminent surgeon and surgical author, born at Dumfries, in 1749,—was educated and practised in Edinburgh, and died in 1806.

Sir Charles Bell, K.H., an eminent anatomist, physiologist, and surgeon,— son of the Reverend William Bell, a clergyman of the Episcopal Church of Scotland, born at Edinburgh in 1774, practised in Edinburgh from 1799 to 1806, when he removed to London, and died in Worcestershire in 1842. He was the author of Anatomy of Expression and the Bridgewater Treatise on the Hand, and other well-known works.

John Bell, elder brother of Sir Charles, also an eminent anatomist and surgeon, born 1763, and died 1820.

George Joseph Bell, also brother of Sir Charles, born 1770, became eminent as a member of the Scottish bar. He was Professor of Law in the Edinburgh University, and one of the principal clerks of the Supreme Court. He died in 1843.

Henry Bell, born at Torphichen, in 1767 ; died at Helensburgh 1830 ; well known for his efforts and success in the introduction of steam navigation.

The Rev. Patrick Bell, of Carmylie, Forfarshire, inventor of a reaping machine.

From the Statistical Account of Scotland we have : " In the Convent of " Carmelites, which was founded by the inhabitants of Jedburgh, lived and died " Adam Bell, Author of Rota Temporum, a History of Scotland from the " earliest times to the year 1535."

Andrew Bell, who had charge of ten thousand sheep of James V, in Ettrick Forest, and gave the King as good an account of them as if they had gone in the bounds of Fife.

The Bells of Hinton, who had a curiously carved pew in the Church of Anworth, with the initials J.B., and date 1631.

Provost Bell, of Dumfries, an. 1740.

Allan Bell, of Hillowtown, parish of Tongland.

John Bell, of Kilduncan, parish of Kingsbarns.

George Bell, of Menslaws, parish of Bedrule ; and many other landed gentlemen.

In Burke we find incidentally mentioned:

James Bell, Surgeon-General of Ireland, 1650—1680.

William Read Bell, of Dorsetshire, circa 1700.

Mathew Bell, of Woolsington.

General Sir John Bell, G.C.B., m. Lady Catherine Harris, eldest daughter of the first Earl of Malmesbury, 1821.

Bell of Sellaby, Co. Durham, circa 1800.

Ralph Bell, of Thirsh, c. 1750.

John Bell, of Bellasis, Middle Marches, c. 1550.

Charles Bell, of Craigfovelie, 1720.

Thomas Bell, of Shortridge, c. 1750.

Henry Bell, of Newbeggin House, Co. Northumberland, c. 1800.

Thomas Bell, Mayor of Dublin, 1702 ; as well as many others.

Of the majority of these little more can be ascertained from the limited sources of information available.

In the churchyard of Kingsbarns there is, or was in 1857, a monument of the Bells of Sandiehill, of which a sketch was taken.

It has been long said in this family that the first of them who settled in Fife, came from Blacketrig or Blackethouse, in Annandale, a trooper or moss-trooper, who did not find it convenient to remain there, after some rebellion (perhaps that in which the house of the Black Douglas fell) ; another version of the tradition has it that he came by way of Ireland, where many of the borderers in the vicinity of the Debateable Land took refuge, or were sent in the 16th century. About the year 1730 the owner of Sandiehill, Andrew Bell, left three properties to his three nephews. Sandiehill to the eldest, whose male descendants are extinct, the land having been long ago sold to the Earl of Kellie, whose footman, about 1823, disposed of a quantity of parchment for measures to a tailor in Kingsbarns. The representative of the second nephew was the late Reverend Dr. Bell, of Linlithgow, whose brothers survive; and from the third, John, who inherited Kilduncan, is descended John Beatson Bell, of Kilduncan and Glenfarg. This third nephew, John Bell, also acquired Bonnytoun, and left it to his second son, David, whose eldest son is now General Sir John Bell, G.C.B. The third son of John Bell of Kilduncan and Bonnytoun, Thomas Bell, of Belmont, settled in Dundee, and was for many years provost of that town. The present Thomas Bell, of Belmont, is his son.

There were also Bells, of Bellfield, near Dundee. They were descended from the Reverend James Bell, of Arbroath, who came about 1745 from Annandale. Of that family the eldest son, Robert, settled in London. and his son William was a partner of Lord Kinnaird in a Dundee bank, and of others in a London Bank. Of his sons one was the traveller in Circassia, and another is the Hon'ble S. S. Bell, Senior Puisne Judge of the Supreme Court at the Cape of Good Hope. John Bell, of Bellfield, was third son of the Rev. James Bell, of Arbroath, and a daughter married a Guthrie of Craigie.

There are also families of Bells of Jamaica, and others whose bearings are mentioned in Burke's General Armoury.

Bell (Jamaica). Az. a fesse engrailed between 3 bells or.—*Crest*—A stag's head erased gu. attired ar. *Motto*—Fulget Virtus.

Bell (Sunderland, Co. Durham). Sa. a chev. erm. betw. 3 church bells ar. *Crest*—A hawk close ppr. beaked and belled or.

Bell (Berkshire and Buckinghamshire). Sa. 3 church bells ar. two and one, and 3 estoiles or. one and two. *Crest*—A hawk with wings expanded ar. beaked and belled or. with a string flotant from the bells gu.

Bell (Essex). Erm. on a chief sa., an escallop shell between two bells ar. *Crest*—A talbot pass. erm.

Bell (Essex). Erm. on a chief sa. three church bells ar.

Bell (Gloucestershire). Ar. on a chev. betw. three hawks' bells gu., two bars gemelles of the first, on a chief of the second a hawk's lure betw. two martlets of the field. *Crest*—An arm embowed vested gu. holding in the hand ppr. a battle ax, staff gu., head ar.

Bell (London). Az. on a chev. ar. between three lions' heads erased or, gorged with a collar of the first, charged with three bezants, as many church bells of the field ornamented of the third.

Bell (London). Sa. a fesse erm. betw. three church bells ar. *Crest*—A human heart between two wings. *Motto*—Forward, kind heart.

Bell (Newcastle). The same. *Crest*—A hawk close ppr. beaked and belled or. *Motto*—Perseverantia.

Bell (Northumberland and Cumberland). Gu. on a chief ar., three church bells sa.

Bell (Westmoreland and Cumberland). Sa. a chev. betw. three church bells ar.

Bell (Scotland). Az. three bells or. *Crest*—A bell or.

Bell (Scotland). The same arms. *Crest*—A demi lion ramp. ppr. *Motto*—Dextra fide que.

Bell (Scotland). The same. *Crest*—An arm in armour grasping a scimitar, all ppr. *Motto*—Pro Rege et Patria.

Bell (Leith). Az. a fesse chequy ar. and sa. between three bells in chief or., and a serpent bent as a crescent in base of the second. *Crest*—A dexter hand with two last fingers folding down ppr. *Motto*—Confido.

Bell (Baughton, Co. Suffolk). Ar. on a chev. engr. or. betw. three talbots' heads erased gu. as many trefoils slipped vert.

Bell (Yorkshire). Sa on a chev. betw. three church bells ar. as many lion's heads couped gu.

Bell. Gu. a fesse erm. betw. three church bells ar. *Crest*—A falcon close belled or. *Motto*—Prend moi tel que je suis.

Bell. Az. a fesse erminois, cottised or. in chief two martlets of the last. *Crest*—On a rock ppr. a martlet erminois.

Bell. Sa. a fesse erm. betw. three mascles (another martlets) ar.

Bell. Az. a fesse betw. three church bells or.

Bell. Sa. a fess erm. betw. three church bells or.

Bell. Per chev. gu and or., a crescent counterchanged.

Bell (Wolsington, Co. Northumberland, represented by Matthew Bell of that place, esq., M.P.) Sa. a fesse erm. betw. three church bells ar.

Bell (Rammerscales, Co. Dumfries). Az. three church bells or. *Crest*—A hand grasping a dagger. *Motto*—I beir the bel.

The Army and Navy lists of bygone years and like works would—with time, opportunity, and inclination—enable any one to swell the records of the name to a formidable size in this manner.

From Hart's Army Lists, for example, we may take:

"Royal Artillery, Major-General ⓑ ⓒⓑ William Bell, a Peninsular and "Waterloo Officer. Major-General Bell's services,—capture of the islands of "St. Thomas and St. Croix in 1807; siege of Fort Desaix, Martinique; capture "of Les Saintes, near Guadaloupe, and bombardment, and driving from the "anchorage the French fleet in 1809; capture of Guadaloupe and adjacent islands "in 1810. Served in the Peninsula and France from July, 1813, to July, 1814, "including the passage of the Bidassoa, Nivelle, Nive, and four days' engage-"ments near Bayonne, passage of the Adour, investment of Bayonne, affairs at "Vic Bagorre and Tarbes, passage of the Garronne, and subsequent operations "to the battle of Toulouse, where he was slightly wounded. Served also the "campaign of 1815, including the battles of Quatre Bras and Waterloo, and "capture of Paris. He has the silver war medal with five clasps."

"4th (The King's Own) Regiment of Foot. Colonel ⓑ Sir John Bell, G.C.B. "General Sir John Bell served in Sicily in 1806 and 1807, in the Peninsula and "France from July, 1808, to Feb., 1809, and again from May, 1809, to July, 1814, "including the battle of Vimiera, action at the bridge of Almeida, battle at "Busaco, all the actions during the retreat of the French from Portugal, siege "and storming of Ciudad Rodrigo, siege and storming of Badajos, action at the "heights of Castrillos, battle of Salamanca, action of Sabijana de Morillos, battles "of Vittoria, the Pyrenees, Nivelle, Orthes, and Toulouse. Served afterwards "with the army employed against Louisiana from Dec., 1814, to June, 1815. He "has received the gold cross for the battles of the Pyrenees, Nivelle, Orthes, and "Toulouse, and the silver war medal with six clasps for the other battles and "sieges." He received the reward for distinguished services, and was for many years one of the aides-de-camp to the Queen. In 1858 he was selected by the Duke of Wellington as Lieutenant-Governor of Guernsey to meet some difficulty in that island, and at the request of the inhabitants he was retained in that position for twice the usual term of the appointment.

"Major Charles Harland Bell, late of the Cape Mounted Rifles, served "throughout the Kafir War of 1850—52 (medal) on the staff of Major-General "Somerset, commanding the first division, and was present in every engagement "with the division; commanded a detachment of Cape Mounted Rifles at the "Kafir attack on Fort Hare and Alice, 21st June, 1851, when the enemy were "repulsed with great loss."

"Bt. Major William Bell, of the 32nd Regt., was present at the battle of "Goojerat (medal and clasps)."

"Lt.-Colonel 𝔓 Thomas Bell, C.B , 48th Regt., and Major-General 𝔓 Edward "Wells Bell, Lieutenant-Governor of Jamaica (1855), both served in the "Peninsula; as also Colonel 𝔓 George Bell, C.B., Imp. F.O., whose name, "in 1855, stands among those of officers receiving rewards for distinguished "services."

These are taken from a mere passing glance at Hart's Army Lists of October, 1855, and January, 1864, the only ones which happen to be at hand. The Indian Service Lists show about fourteen Bells. Many more might be found in the Navy Lists, Home and Colonial Civil Lists, &c.; but enough has at present been noted to point the way to any clansman, with more inclination and more liesure and means at his disposal.

Popular poetry, too, has indirectly made us acquainted with the Laird of Kinvaid, in Perthshire. Who has not heard of his daughter and her friend,

> "Bessie Bell and Mary Gray?
> They were twa bonnie lasses,
> They biggit a bouir on yon burn brae,
> And theekit it o'er wi' rashes,"

as a refuge from the plague, which a lover was, nevertheless, the means of communicating to them from Perth in 1666, or some other year shortly before it, if, as is asserted, the great plague of London was not that which ravaged Scotland. Anyhow, the young ladies died,

> "They thocht to rest in Methven Kirk,
> Amang their gentle kin,
> But they maun lie on Lednoch braes,
> To beek forenent the sun."

## 𝔅.

### "Bells of Tinwald."

The List under "Elleventh Parliament of King James the Sext, xxix of Julij, 1587," gives the name of the Clan, and indicates that, even down to that date, the Bells were under Patriarchal Chiefs rather than Feudal Superiors.

There is first "The Roll of the Names of the Landislords and Baillies "of Landes dwelling on the Bordours and in the Hielandes, quhair broken "men hes dwelt, and presently dwellis. To the quhilk Roll, the 95 Acte of "this Parliament is relative.

### "Middle March.

"The Earle of Bothwell.

"The Laird of Fairniehirst.

"The Earl of Augus," &c., &c , &c.

Then follows, " The Rolle of the Clannes that hes Captaines and Chieftaines, " quhom on they depende, oftimes against the willes of their Landes Lordes, " alsweill on the Bordoures, as Hielandes, and of sum special persons of " Braunches of the saidis Clannes.

### " Middle Marche.

" Ellotes.
" Arme Stranges.
" Nicksonnes.
" Crosers.

### " West Marche

" Scottes of Eusdaill.
" Beatisonnes.
" Littles.
" Thomsonnes.
" Glendunninges.
" Irvinges.
" Belles.
" Carrutheres.
" Grahames.
" Johnstones.
" Jardanes.
" Moffettes.
" Latimers.

### " Hielandes and Iles.

" Buchannanes.
" Mak-farlanes of the Arroquhair," &c., &c.

The following complete return will better show, comparatively, the fighting strength of " the Belles."

From Bell's MS. introduction to History of Cumberland (Nicholson, p. 65).

### Annerdale.

| | |
|---|---|
| Laird of Kirkmighel | 222 |
| ——— Rose | 165 |
| ——— Hempsfield | 163 |
| ——— Homeends | 162 |
| ——— Wamphray | 102 |
| ——— Dunwoodij | 44 |
| ——— Newby and Gratney | 122 |
| ——— Tinnel (Tinwald) | 102 |
| Patrick Murray | 203 |
| Christie Urwin (Irvine), of Coreshaw. | 102 |
| Cuthbert Urwin, of Robbsgill | 34 |
| Urwins of Sennersack. | 40 |
| Wat Urwen.. | 20 |

| | |
|---|---|
| Jeffrey Urwen........................ | 93 |
| T. Johnston, of Craikburn............................ | 64 |
| James Johnstone, of Coits............................ | 162 |
| Johnstones, of Craggyland ....  ............ | 37 |
| Johnstons, of Driesdell............................ | 46 |
| Johnstons, of Mallinshaw............................ | 65 |
| Gawin Johnston............................ | 31 |
| Will Johnston, the Laird's Brother............ | 110 |
| Robin Johnston, of Lochmaben............ | 67 |
| Laird of Gillersbie............................ | 30 |
| Moffits............................ | 24 |
| Bells of Tostints............................ | 142 |
| Bells of Tindills............................ | 222 |
| Sir John Lawson............................ | 32 |
| Town of Annan............................ | 33 |
| Room of Tordephe............................ | 32 |

### Nithsdale.

| | |
|---|---|
| Mr. Maxwell and more............................ | 1000 |
| Laird of Closeburn........  ............ | 403 |
| ———— Lag............................ | 202 |
| ———— Cransfield............................ | 27 |
| Mr. Ed. Creighton............................ | 10 |
| Laird of Cowhill........  ............  ............ | 91 |
| Maxwells of Brackenside and Vicar of Carlaverick..... | 310 |

### Annerdale and Galway.

| | |
|---|---|
| Lord Carlisle............................ | 101 |

### Annerdale and Clidsdale.

| | |
|---|---|
| Laird of Applegirth............................ | 242 |

### Liddesdale and Debateable Land.

| | |
|---|---|
| Armstrongs............................ | 300 |
| Elwoods (Elliots)............................ | 74 |
| Nixons......  ............ | 32 |

### Galloway.

| | |
|---|---|
| Laird of Dowbaillie............................ | 41 |
| Orcherton............................ | 111 |
| Carlisle............................ | 206 |
| Loughenwar............................ | 45 |
| Tutor of Bombie............................ | 140 |
| Abbot of New Abbey............................ | 141 |
| Town of Dumfries............................ | 201 |
| Town of Kirkcubrie............................ | 36 |

## Tividale.

Laird of Drumlire............................. .................. 364
Caruthers........................................................ 71
Trumbells ............... ........................................ 12

## Eskdale.

Battisons and Thomsons.................................. 166

Total 7008 men, under English assurance.

# CONCLUDING NOTE.

MANY very good suggestions have been offered by those who have seen these notes as they passed the press, but too late to admit of convenient alterations being made.

It is objected that conclusions have been jumped at in the case of John Bell, of Antermony (notes A and R), and that the date of 1692 assigned to the manuscript is not thereby affected,—for the celebrated traveller, born in 1691, might have had a father or grandfather of the same name, and of Antermony, as stated. Very true indeed ; but others must solve the question, if it requires solution.

Then, again, as to the latter part of note X, it is remarked that as the Bells were known to have been settled for many generations at Kinvaid, before the first Lord Nairne bought their lands, and long before the bonny Bessie Bell biggit her rash theekit bouir and died on Lednoch braes, the letter from Argyle, Ruthven, and the Regent Murray, of 1560, to Arntully and Kinvaid should not be omitted merely because the name of Bell is not mentioned. The original appears to be in the Regent Murray's own handwriting ; a copy is found in the Statistical Account of Scotland 1798, and whoever may be shown to have been then the Laird of Kinvaid, here it is :

"To our traist friendis, the Lairds of Arntilly and Kinvaid.—Traist friendis, "after maist hearty commendacion, we pray yow faill not to pass incontinent to "the kyrk of Dunkeld, and tak doun the haill images thereof, and bring furth "to the kyrk-zayrd and burn thaym oppinly. And siclyk cast down the altaris, "and purge the kyrk of all kynd of monuments of idolatrye. And this ze faill "not to do, as ze will do us singular emplesenr ; and so committis you to the "protection of God. From Edinburgh the xii of August, 1560.

"Faill not, bot ze tak guid heyd          (Signed)          "AR. ERGYLL,
"that neither the dasks, windocks,                                    "JAMES STEWART,
"nor durris be ony ways hurt                                          "RUTHVEN."
"or broken ———— eyther
"glassin wark or iron wark."

F

The old Castle of Kinvaid, the home of "Bessy Bell," the companion of "Mary Gray," seemed—according to the old Statistical Account (parish of Monedie, co. Perth)—to have been built before lime was known as a cement; but it has now quite disappeared. Mary Gray was daughter of the Laird of Lednoch (now Lynedoch) an adjoining estate to Kinvaid. Their deaths took place 1645.

There are various other scraps which have turned up irregularly, such as that Peter Bell commanded the *Pettyr of Grymysby*, one of the vessels which conveyed the French Queen and the Duke of Suffolk to France, A.D. 1515.

In 1516, among the complaints against the Duke of Albany, are: 2nd, for the murder of Robert Herrison, of the Trowghe of Levin, an Englishman, 10th August last, by various Irwins, John Bell, Rynne Bell, and others. 3rd, murder of Robert Blackborn, of Byrk-Tymber-Hill, an Englishman, 20th November last, by Wat Bell, of Dolphin Flat, White Will Bell, John Bell, Rynne Bell, John Bell, of the Cowshot Hill, David Bell, of Mylnepeth, George Irwin, the twin, &c, with others to the number of 100 Scotch, who burnt the village of Byrk-Tymber-Hill, and drove away 60 kye and oxen, 10 horse, 100 sheep, 40 gate, and the insight of the village.

In 1517, there was one Master Bell, Dean of Arches, recommended by Silvester, Bishop of Worcester, to Andreas Ammonius, Latin Secretary to Henry VIII, as somewhat fit for the Mastership of the English Hospital (of the Knights at Rhodes?) in the following terms: "Thomas Coleman, Master of the "English Hospital, is dead. There are no persons fit to succeed him. The "Bishop of Leghlin is an idle voluptuary, Pencut is a fool, John Grigh stupid, "and the Suffragan of London unfit from his ignorance of the language. Thinks "Master Bell, now Dean of Arches, a more suitable person.'

Again : "Master John Gryghe, who professes to be a servant of Canterbury, "is very urgent to be admitted ma e una bestia et matto publico, come Magistro "Bello vi puo informare, et poco nostro amico."

In 1624 there was a Captain Henry Bell who wrote to Secretary Conway for a company, having been promised it, and having spent £900 in His Majesty's service, &c., &c.

In 1627, probably the same person asserts that he came from Germany in 1617, with £3000 and a recommendation from the Emperor in his pocket, and spent all in services for which he was granted a pension of £500 a-year, of which he had never received a penny. In 1634 is found, probably the same, a victim of the Star Chamber, commencing on the 1st July with a petition to Archbishop Laud, and following it up with other applications for release for years.

Among many other notes, lastly, is observed Captain Sygnolphue Bell, with the oddest christian name ever bestowed on any of the clan, so far as is known. Those inclined to serve the States-General, under Colonel the Earl of Oxford, were referred by Royal proclamation, in 1624, to Captain Sygnolphue Bell at his lodging in the Strand.

In note I, page 25, there is a slip of the pen, viz., "*Kirkconnel, true to his Chief.*" Douglas may have been the Feudal Superior of Kirkconnel, but he never was his Chief, nor could have been Chief of the Bells.

An early number of *Chambers's Journal* gives the following opinion, with Johnsonian gravity,

" To publish a book avowedly imperfect is an insult to the public."

There is no rule without an exception; and even if this be a rule, it cannot apply to a few pages, not published, but merely printed for those of the name of Bell, or connected with it, whose idiosyncracies are such as may be tickled by speculations on its origin, or who may be tempted for the amusement of an idle hour, or as relaxation from more useful employments, to make further attempts to see through the very thick cloud that envelopes the early history of the Clan, whether it arose from the burning of the Blackethouse papers by Cromwell's troopers or otherwise.

There is no idea of claiming any prominent leading position for the name, but it may be shown that it was gentle at an early date after the fashion of bearing hereditary surnames became common, although at its best those who bore it seem to have been always subordinate to one or other of the greater Barons. None of the Clan appear to have ever risen to the rank of Nobles of the land, or to have been in any way great national leaders. It is not known that any of them ever held a fief in capite,—that is, directly of the Sovereign, and probably the letter of safe conduct in the 29th year of Henry the VI is the best voucher of the early respectability and standing of the Chief that can be adduced.

Here the subject must necessarily be dropped, at all events for the present,— still with the hope that there are among us many much more capable, in every way, of following up the track, who will try to do so, and to contradict whatever may have been herein stated in error. There must be many with abilities and opportunities sufficient to enable them to collect, for preservation and distribution among us, drawings or photographs of such relics as the grave-stones in Middlebie Kirkyard, or any others, illustrative of the results of further investigation.

There is nothing to be said of the value or importance of such inquiries. Neither to the utilitarian nor to any other sneerer at supposed fools gleaning mere food for family pride and personal vanity in such a field, forgetting how ridiculous it is to claim credit, as if for a choice of progenitors whose standing it may be difficult to maintain, and whose acknowledged virtues and brighter merits may overcast with a dirtier shade, but can never whitewash, any stains on their descendants' own reputation. Much of such folly exists, no doubt of it; but such sneering men of the world fairly expose themselves to the contempt of deeper thinkers, if, in deference to prevailing fashion, they affect to repress entirely or utterly ignore that natural hankering after knowledge of ancestry, implanted in the human breast by the same hand that wrote on stone amid the thunders of Sinai,

"Honour thy father and thy mother."

Who dares confess himself so utterly sunk in brutish selfishness as not to wish to look up to or look back to his parents with veneration, nor to care for the fair fame of brother or sister, or that his own children should recollect and respect him? It is merely an extension of the opposite feeling that prompts the Scot to look a little further with a peculiar interest to his grandparents and their forebears, to his cousins and their clan. Should any worthy clansman meet a man believed—really believed—to have nothing of this in him, mark him and beware of him. He would sell his country, betray his friend, and foul his own nest for a price.

There is, of course, a reasonable limit to the rigid application of these remarks, and it is not to be insisted on that every one should trouble himself very much about one or two out of his fifty thousand ancestors buried five hundred years ago. It may, perhaps, even be somewhat excusable to regard such remote ancestors with no greater interest than any of their contemporary fellow-countrymen, and some otherwise very intelligent and right-feeling people would not give a fig for a complete collection of the veritable baptismal certificates and marriage lines of every one of them. In fact, it would be rather dry reading; and otherwise it is obvious that common delicacy prescribes the desk or the farthest library shelf, rather than the drawing-room table, as the proper place for all books of genealogy or history of the family and connexions of the household.

Most of the middle classes may be quite content with the ancestry of a very few respectable generations; yet this manuscript, and these notes, may enable some to link on their own pedigrees to one or more of the branches of the Clan mentioned therein,—and it is hoped the subject will amuse them, and others for whom these pages are intended.

If the said pages circulate more widely, be it hereby known, it is under protest; but if any kindly clansman will collect other scraps that may be within his reach, or pleases to work up the foregoing with a collection of his own, he is requested to send a copy (if letter-press half-a-dozen copies) addressed to B., under cover to the printers of this pamphlet, a firm as enterprising and liberal as any in Father Land or Mother Country,—Saul Solomon & Co., Printers and Publishers, Government Gazette Office, Cape Town, Cape of Good Hope.